E

M

The Boy Who Could Make

His Mother Stop Yelling

Published by Rainbow Press

Text copyright © 1982 by Ilse Sondheimer

Illustrations copyright © 1982 by dee deRosa

The text is 18 point Garamond Light.
Printed by M.C. Printing Co., Syracuse, N.Y.
Library of Congress Catalog Card No. 81-86219

2   3   4   5   6   7   8   9   10   11   12

ISBNO-943156-00-9

For Susan and Ellen
I.S.

For Susie
d.deR.

The Boy Who Could Make

His Mother Stop Yelling

by Ilse Sondheimer
illustrated by dee deRosa

RAINBOW PRESS
222 Edwards Drive
Fayetteville, N.Y. 13066

The boy was Danny,

and his mother was
a very, very big lady.

She had two great big arms

in which she held

Danny's new baby brother;

and she had two voices.

One was soft

like a blue blanket,

and she used it

to say to Danny's baby brother,

"Don't you worry, little one,

you'll get your bottle in just one

minute."

Her other voice was big,

like a lion's,

and she used it for Danny

when she said,

"How many times

do I have to tell you

not to leave

your new tricycle outside?

It would serve you right

if somebody came along

and took it.

And I TOLD YOU

that it'll get rusty

if you keep leaving it

out in the rain."

So Danny went outside

and wiped the rain

off his new tricycle

and brought it up on the porch.

And then his mother said,

in her big lion voice,

"Did you use

a BATHTOWEL TO WIPE IT?

Oh, Danny, you know

where the rags are!"

Danny went into his room.

He built a big cage with his blocks.

Then he wanted to go out to play,

but his mother said,

"Not now,

it's still drizzling out."

But when Danny's marbles

fell on the floor

and the baby started to cry again,

she said, "Maybe if

you put on your raincoat

you could go out

for a while."

Danny went to the closet —

no raincoat;

he looked under his bed —

no raincoat.

He looked by the backdoor —

no raincoat.

He even checked the bathroom.

And then he was sure

that his mother would yell again

because he had left

his raincoat in school.

Danny started to cry,

and that's when

the strange thing happened.

His mother,

who was so big,

started to cry too.

She said, "Oh, Danny!

I just don't know

what to do any more,"

and then she cried harder

and harder.

All of a sudden

Danny knew what he could do.

He climbed on his mother's lap

and held her very tight.

He said, "If you only wouldn't use

that great big lion voice,

I'd bring in my tricycle,

and not wake up the baby."

His mother stopped crying.

"You would," she asked,

"if I wouldn't yell at you?"

"Sure," said Danny,

and he could tell

that his own voice sounded

very grown up,

"and when the baby gets bigger

I'll show him how to

pick up his blocks

and put them away."

"All right,"

said Danny's mother,

"then I'll try to remember,

I really will,

about my great big lion voice."